THE YOUNG LOST LADY

JERMEL ARCILICIA TAYLOR

Jermel's Raison D'être
Copyright © 2013 by Jermel's Raison D'être Publishing
www.jermelsraisondetre.com

All rights reserved. No part of this book may be reproduced or transmitted in any form or by any means without written permission from the author.

ISBN-13 978-0-9893179-1-7
Printed in USA

Table of Contents

Opening Remarks	6
Chapter 1	10
Chapter 2	20
Chapter 3	29
Chapter 4	40
Chapter 5	48
Chapter 6	57
Chapter 7	63
Chapter 8	68
Chapter 9	74
Chapter 10	78
Chapter 11	82
Chapter 12	88
Chapter 13	93

Chapter 14	98
Chapter 15	102
Chapter 16	105
Closing Remarks	107
Author's Bio	108

Dedicated to Thessodena Taylor. With God and hard work, all things are possible. Everything I do is because of you.

In loving memory to those that died homegrown in K-Town. They will be truly missed. Until we meet again. Love ya'll.

Opening Remarks

La-dy [ley-dee] –noun 1. A woman who is refined, polite, and well-spoken: She may be poor and have little education.

2. A woman of high social position or economic class: She was born a lady and found it hard to adjust to her reduced circumstances.

3. Slang. A female lover or steady companion.

When one is born into the world, you are considered female when you have the XX chromosomes. Everybody is happy because a female is a big asset to the world, for they are the bearers of life meaning without the female, the human species would not be in existence; which also means, the infant female will eventually have to grow in to a woman and hopefully becoming a lady.

But the real question is, what is a lady and who defined being a lady? Was it the way she walked, talked, dressed or who she slept with? Who decided the rules of becoming a lady anyway? Isn't it after a certain age you are allowed to do what you want? If there are rules to becoming or being a lady, who teachers her how to be a lady? Her mother can teach her what she believes a lady should be, but if she has different men and in her life at one time, is that a lady? What if her mother believes this is a lady because of what she learned from her mother, and her mother could have learned her ways from her mother with a repeating cycle; is it then ok?

On the other hand, if the girl has a father in her household or in her life, he can teach her what being a lady is from a man's point of view. Her father will always want the best for his daughter. Even if he is unfaithful to his partner, he will not want his daughter being with someone that will be unfaithful to her. He will try his best to teach her how a man should teach his princess if he is in his right mind. That is man law. Is that right? She might listen to him, but her actions might speak differently because of his actions.

Living in the ghetto and trying to become a man is challenging, but trying to blossom into a lady, is erratic. Everything seems harder on a female. Females have to worry about so many coerce things. They say what you see is your reality and if that is correct, having babies, drinking, smoking, and hustling is it. To become a lady you have to have a whole different mind frame. Males convey the impression that they can do what they want and get away with it. Males don't have a limit to how many sex partners they have in the eyes of the ghetto because that's the cool thing to do. Why is it like this? Who knows, but it seems like society dictates everything, so for society, to be considered a lady, you can't have a certain piece of clothing on, or sleep with a certain amount of men. If you do, you are considered a whore.

By cause of what was just said, being lost or off track, of course, is a mental condition. It associates with being unaware, confused, and emotionally unstable. It doesn't matter race, color, age, or creeds. After the mental condition has set in, the environment plays the rest of the role. The mental condition of a lost female is very complex which is the reason why certain actions cannot be explained.

With that, this is a fictitious story, but relates to real life situations. Certain behaviors of the characters might not be relatable because of the environment. Also, every case scenario is different.

In closing, read this story with an unblocked mind. Try to place yourself in the main characters shoes. No person is perfect.

Chapter 1

It's a bright and warm summer morning in Waukegan, Illinois. The birds are chirping and the water sprinklers are on in all the front lawns. Marie is in the kitchen of her big house preparing breakfast for her and her two granddaughters, Nichole and Danielle while mentally preparing for her weekend.

"Girls…. Girls…." Marie shouts out to get their attention.

"Come down stairs. It's time to eat breakfast. Don't let the food get cold girls," she says while sitting at the table drinking her orange juice.

Marie is sixty five and her voice is so strong it probably awoke the neighbors. With the sun beaming down in the kitchen, Marie is ready to eat and get her day started. Seeing the girls makes the beginning of her day well.

"I'm coming Granny," Danielle utters back from upstairs. Barely opening her eyes, Danielle sticks her feet outside of the cover feeling the cold air sweep across her bare feet onto the soft carpet on the floor.

Before she stands up, Danielle catches her last few Z's sitting on the side of her bed. Today is not a school day but the day to go with mommy and daddy. Danielle is always excited about going with daddy and mommy but she is exhausted from playing in heaven or the backyard all yesterday after school.

Danielle wants to fall backwards into the bed and go back to sleep when her older sister Nichole runs into the room screaming, "Wake up Danielle, we go with mommy and daddy today.

"I know Nichole. Get out my room." Danielle says acting like she is fully awoke.

Danielle puts her all into getting herself up while forcing her eyelids open. She staggers out of her room heading for the bathroom before she reaches her destination, Nichole jumps out the linen closet trying to scare her.

"Boo!" Nichole says loud and fast.

"Girl, it's too early in the morning for you to be playing. You act like the little sister. I think I'm older than you."

"Whatever. I'm just trying to wake you up because you was sleep walking," Nichole says skipping away.

Danielle loves her sister but sometimes she just wants to punch her in the face. Nichole plays a lot but she does wake Danielle up. Danielle uses the bathroom and heads down stairs. When she reaches the kitchen, granny and Nichole are at the table.

"Nice to have you join us Danielle." Marie says with a smile on her face.

"Good morning granny," she says while sticking her tongue out at Nichole.

She sits at the table and waits until granny puts the food on her plate.

"You girls have to eat up now because your daddy and mommy will be here soon."

"Granny, did you cook bacon?" Nichole asks.

"Yes, I did baby."

"Did you cook eggs granny?"

"Yes baby," Marie says with a smile

"With cheese too?" Nichole asks passionately.

"Why you ask so many questions?" Danielle interrupts without looking for an answer.

"Stop it girls," Marie says sternly.

"Yes Nichole. I put cheese in the eggs," Answering Nichole's question calmly.

"Yay, I love cheese in my eggs granny," Nichole says while rocking side to side in her seat getting herself ready to eat.

"I know you do baby." Marie says in comfort.

    Marie and the girls sit at the brown round table to enjoy breakfast. Marie makes sure the girls eat early before they go with their parents, Bo and Lynn. The girls are always excited to see their parents because they don't see them often, so it's minimum talk; they eat in a hurry. When they are done eating, they rush upstairs to change from pajamas to outside clothes.

"Make sure you girls brush your tongue," she says while cleaning the table off.

"Yes granny," the girls yell back happily.

Marie loves her grandkids. Before they came to live with her, life was routine. The girls added the spark she needed. They make her feel good inside and out.

Upstairs, the girls are franticly getting dressed. Nichole is looking for her favorite shirt while singing her favorite song. She finds it fairly quickly. Danielle is in her room looking for her favorite Barbie doll, Babee. Danielle dislikes leaving home without Babee. She looks all over the room; after a while she finds Babee under the bed. Now she can get dressed.

In the process of the girls getting dressed, the door bell rings.

"Ding Dong"

"Mommy," Danielle screams out in high spirit.

"Finish up girls and come downstairs. Your mommy is here." Marie shouts to the girls.

Lynn comes in and sits on the flowered covered living room sofa. She looks a little exhausted but she tries not to show it.

"Hi momma," Lynn says dully while staring at her childhood pictures.

"Good morning Lynn. I hope that you are taking care of yourself. Those girls need you to be healthy. I'm not going to be here forever." Marie says in concernment.

"Momma, I'm fine and my girls will be fine if you die. I hate when you talk like that." Lynn responds.

"Ok, I'm just making sure because I don't want anything to happen to them."

"Ok momma. You know I'm getting myself together and…"

While the two are talking, the girls come downstairs with the biggest smiles on their faces.

"Mommy," the girls scream out in unison.

They hug their mom tight making it appear as though they haven't seen her in years. Lynn and the girls get reacquainted for a short while. Soon after, they tell their grandmother they love her and head out the door.

Lynn and the girls walk to the car where Bo is inside waiting on them. The girls get into the backseat. Their greeting to Bo is a little mild compared to their mothers greeting.

"Hi daddy," the girls say.

"Hey girls! Daddy is glad to see ya'll. I love ya'll," Bo says in an upbeat manner.

"We love you too daddy," the girls respond unexcited.

Bo smiles at the girls and drives off. In the back seat, Danielle and Nichole start talking to each other about the fun they are going to have over the weekend while Bo and Lynn start conversing with each other about where they will be staying for the weekend because when the girls go with their parents, they don't go to their house, they go to a one room, two bed hotel. It's never the same hotel, but always the same set up.

Bo and Lynn always try to find a hotel in or close to Waukegan. Before they check into one, they always stop by a store to buy the girls a new toy to play with. They want to be good parents. When they find a hotel they will stay in for the weekend, they give the girls their bed and they take theirs.

"Ya'll take that bed and that side of the room," Bo tells the girls.

He continues, "I will turn the T.V. to that side and ya'll can watch cartoons while me and ya'll momma stay on this side."

"Yes Daddy," the girls reply.

Staying on their side is what the girls do. They don't go outside to play. They play all of their games on the floor on the side of their bed. They don't go outside to eat. Bo and Lynn orders food for pick up. The girls don't mind because they are use to eating home cooked meals at home. The thing the girls don't like is when after they eat, Bo and Lynn start to do strange things on their side of the room. The sounds of sparks are sharp seconds later the room gets filled with smoke which has a weird smell to it that makes Danielle tummy hurts. It doesn't bother Nichole.

Danielle tries to cover her nose when the smoke is in the room, but her stomach always windup hurting. This time it's worse than others. The smoke doesn't last long in the room, but after the smoke clears, things almost go back to normal until Bo and Lynn starts to fight. Bad words are the beginning of their fighting. It appears that the smoke turns Bo into a different person. It starts with "Bitch I run this."

All at once the bad words leads up to Bo beating on Lynn for an extended period of time. Bo usually chokes and punches Lynn in the face until he tires himself out.

While this goes on, the girls hide behind the bed hoping a wall forms between the two beds. While hiding, the girls peak over it wishing that they could stop their daddy from beating on mommy, but crying is all they can do.

Right after Bo is done beating Lynn, he makes up to the girls by taking them out to eat or buying them a new toy. The girls are ok with this because they know that their daddy loves them. Bo knows that when he takes them out, the girls will forget all about the beating he gives Lynn but the reality is that the girls will never forget.

When the weekend is up, Bo and Lynn take the girls back to Marie's house. Lynn tries to avoid her mother after every weekend, so she lets them out in the front of the house and leaves. The girls always want to stay with their parents, but they have to go back to granny's house. They don't cry they just get back to their ordinary life.

Chapter 2

Since the girls are at home with Marie, they don't have a worry in the world. The things that they see when they go with their parents, they don't think about, but Marie does. Marie knows what her daughter does and she doesn't like it. This is why she does everything in her power to make the girls happy. Whatever the girls want, they get. The absence of pain is Marie's number one pledge.

The backyard was the main investment to keep everybody happy. For Nichole and Danielle, it's a fully loaded playground. The girls can do everything from climb the monkey bars, to the feeling of flying on the swing, or sliding down the slide like one does from the top of a hill to the bottom; all smiles. It's their heaven. Marie loves watching the girls play in their gym, it's her bliss.

For herself, she has The Garden. It's located in the rear of the backyard so the girls won't have a reason to distort it. She grows everything from tomatoes, onions, greens, carrots, garlic and a few other table vegetables. Marie puts much effort into The Garden because she is very particular about her veggies, so the tomatoes are always the reddest and the greens the freshest; so remarkable.

Marie has been nurturing Nichole and Danielle since they were two and three, but now they are nine and ten. They can be a handful at times, but Marie would like to see them go to high school and if she's blessed enough, college, but now, she has to consider making a life changing decision.

The girls are with their parents, and Marie is at home alone working in The Garden on a hot sunny day. While she is putting some tomatoes in her basket, she hears the doorbell. She answers the door. It's her younger sister Alice who really acts like the older sister after all these years. The visit is casual at first. While walking back to The Garden, the two start their conversing.

"Hello Marie. How are you doing?" Alice asks a sarcastic type way.

"I'm blessed. How are you doing Alice?"

"I'm fair....but I'm worried about you Marie," Alice says.

"Why are you worried about me Alice?"

While Marie is waiting on her answer she puts her gloves back on and kneel so she can finish what she started back in The Garden.

"Well, I'm fine," Marie says while putting tomatoes in her basket.

"You didn't give me time to answer your question Marie. But I'm concerned about you. I know you love those girls, but shouldn't you have a life too?"

Interrupting her, "I have a life Alice. They are my life."

"I'm just saying Marie. You have worked your whole life, you deserve a break now. You've raised your kids…..let her raise hers." Alice says while staring at the back of Marie's head.

Marie doesn't respond to Alice for a short while then she stops what she is doing to say, "I really don't know what to say to this. I know you are not saying this to get ahead with anything. I know you are concerned about me, well at least I hope you are really concerned about me, but do you really think Lynn can handle raising those girls?

"That is something she has to do and figure out as a mother; we did it. She has to pray away all those bad habits to be a good mother," Alice says.

"You bring up a good point, but those girls don't need that around them…..I just don't know," She says while wiping her head free of sweat.

"I know how you feel, but really think about it… please Marie. You deserve a life," Alice says.

The two finish up the conversation with a hug and a kiss on the cheek.

While walking out the door, Alice says "It's your life nonetheless, so you do what you want to. Love you big sis."

"Love you too Alice," Marie responds.

Letting her sister out the house gives a relief. She knows her sister cares, but what about the girls?

They didn't ask to be here. Since they are here, don't they deserve a good life? Marie tries her hardest to cut off the thoughts about her giving the girls back to Lynn. She finds things to do in the house to get her mind off the situation; Cleaning, eating, pacing, and praying. The girls come back tomorrow, so it's really hard for her not to think about it. With a slight feel of depression, Marie prepares for bed.

The hotel room that the girls are in this weekend is much smaller than the others. There is only one bed and Bo and Lynn are in it sleep. The girls are lying on the brown carpeted floor next to the wall. Since it is bedtime, it is pitch black in the room. The floor is cold as ice and the girls only have one sheet and pillow. Full of pain, Danielle is forcing herself to sleep but is unable too, so she touches her sister to see if she is up.

"Nichole, you sleep?" She asks.

"No, I'm up. What you want?"

"I wonder why daddy always hitting mommy?"

"I think it's the stuff he smokes and drinks." Nichole whispers.

"I love daddy, but I hate it when he hits mommy,"

"Girl be quiet before you wake daddy up," Nichole says while covering Danielle's mouth.

Danielle mumbles some gibberish under breathe while Nichole over talks her. "I hate it too, but that's our daddy. Don't wake him up so he can beat us too. Keep quiet, ok?"

Slowly removing her hand from Danielle's mouth, the two pause for a short while then suddenly Danielle starts to cry.

"Girl stop all that crying," Nichole demands.

"I can't cus I wish….I just wish." Danielle isn't able to finish what she was saying.

    The beating that she saw Bo give her mother earlier today hurt like none-other. She is scared for her mom. She is also confused. Something is growing inside of Danielle; something troubled, something rebellious. All she can do is cry in Nichole's arms until she falls into a nippy sleep; Nicole follows her lead.

The girls wake up to the smell of breakfast appearing like nothing happened last night. Bo serves the girls food, eggs and bacon, on the floor while the two eat at the table in the corner. In the time when everyone is eating, Danielle starts to look over at her mom to see her face. Danielle tries to get a glimpse of Lynn's swollen eye when she turns and hide like they are playing pick-a-boo.

When Bo sees this, he instantly tell the girls "Hurry up and eat that food so ya'll can go back to grandma house."

"Yes daddy."

The girls finish eating, gather up their things, and follow Bo to the car. Lynn stays behind.

Marie is having a long night because she can't sleep. Tossing and turning followed along with long periods of staring at the brown ceiling fan by cause of reoccurring scenes of the girls smiling, laughing, and playing while living with her is keeping her awake. She is also forcefully thinking about what her sister was said about letting the girls go back to Lynn.

Marie's thoughts are all over the place. She needs to gather some order. Maybe she can if she gets coffee. She looks over at the alarm clock and it shows 5:45 am. With a slight feel of disbelief, she gets up, goes to the bathroom to clean herself then proceeds to the kitchen. Marie enters the kitchen in a sluggish manner slowly removing the coffee out the cabinet while considering the decision she feels she has to make. Preparing her coffee, she thinks to herself as of lately, it has appeared that Lynn has it easy and is doing whatever she wants. It might be time for Lynn to have some real responsibility.

With the smell of brewing coffee in the air, she asks herself, *why is that Lynn gets to run around with Bo doing whatever she pleases?* It's not right. *She thinks she slick.* Shaking her head, she makes her coffee. While putting the necessary ingredients in, she notices how peaceful her house is without the girls.

She has sudden insight; an epiphany. She wants to live the rest of her life kid-less.

    While staring out of the window into the clouds, she decides enough is enough. She is going to let the girls go back to Lynn. She has already proven her parenthood. She can't help if Lynn is the way she is. God knows she did her best. Maybe the girls will wake Lynn up, and slow her down because she did her part.

Chapter 3

Bo and the girls head to Marie's house. There is complete silence in the car. All Danielle is thinking about is her mom. Flashbacks of Bo hitting her mom is replaying in her mind. A part of her wants to jump in the front seat and hurt him like he hurts her mom. The other part of her doesn't want to touch him. He makes her sick.

When they arrive at Marie's house, Bo puts on a front while helping the girls out of the car.

"Ok girls. We are here. Let me help you girls get out." He says.

Nichole accepts his help. Danielle on the other hand jumps back to the other side of the car like she saw a snake.

"What's wrong Danielle? What you see? Bo asks.

She is quiet. She wants to scream but something is holding her back; similar to something holding her mouth. She stares at him. Bo tries again. She jumps back again.

"Nichole, tell your sister to get out that car before I come get her," he says in a irritating manner. Nichole crawls back into the car to talk to her sister.

"Come on girl. Let's go in the house with grandma. He is not going to touch you right now." Nichole says while holding her hand out. "But if you don't, he is too," she finish saying. Danielle stares for a while then grabs her hand and gets out of the car. She walks to the house on the opposite side of Nichole to avoid standing by Bo. He tries to reach over to hold her hand but she moves it.

They reach the door and Bo gives them a look like they better not say a thing about their weekend. Marie answers the door with a smile on her face. She knows she has made a very important decision but her peace of mind prevents her from showing it.

The girls enter, hug Marie and go to their rooms. Bo returns the smile and gets ready to turn around and walk away when Marie gets his attention, "Bo, where is my daughter?" She asks.

Bo turns around slowly, "Um, she stayed back this morning so she could sleep. She wasn't feeling well."

"Ok. Can you tell her to call me? I have something important to tell her." Marie says.

"Yes maa'm. I will tell her soon as I get back," he says turning and walking off.

While the girls are upstairs freshening up, Marie stays downstairs pacing back and forth thinking of how she is going to tell Lynn to get a hold of the girls. In the time she is coming up with the script, the girls are upstairs running, jumping, and making lots of noise. Looking at the white ceiling shaking her head, she tells herself, *this is the reason why I can't take it anymore.*

Driving back to the hotel, he wonders what it is she has to tell Lynn. If she wants to give the girls back, he has to get the hell out of dodge. He wants to do his own thing anyway. He doesn't want to be tied down with those kids. Giving the car gas, his thoughts are all over the place. His hands are sweating profusely. He's in a frantic state, but then he asks himself, *what if I don't tell her? I can keep her from picking the girls up. Na, that won't work. She has to get them sooner or later. No matter what she decides, I ain't going to be tied down.... I don't even know what it is yet. I'm tripping and shit. I need to leave them drugs alone. Shits getting to me.*

He reaches the hotel where Lynn lay's across the bed.

"Aye woman," he say's sternly.

"Yea," she says awakening from her slumber.

"Yo mamma said she wants to talk to you about something important. I hope she not trying to give them girls back to you."

Wiping the sleep from her swollen eye, she slowly sits up.

"She didn't say what it was or what she wanted?"

"No woman. She just said she wanted to talk to about something important in person. That's it," he answers.

"I don't want to go over there with my eye like this."

"Put some ice on that shit," he says immediately.

He continues, "After that, put some sunglasses on and see what she wants."

She finishes stretching and proceeds to follow his orders. While she is sitting on the side of the bed with ice on her face, she thinks to herself that she could just call Marie. It makes better since. She calls Marie to what's so important, but Marie wouldn't tell her. Marie insists that she comes over. Since there is no way around it, she waits for a few days until her eye un-swells.

After a few days, her eye goes down well and she goes to Marie house, but she still wears her sunglasses. She doesn't bring Bo with her. She takes the bus alone. When she reaches the house, the girls are in the backyard and Marie is in the front yard waiting on her with a look on her face that can burn a hole through a wall. This automatically gives Lynn a feel of concern, so every step she takes, she thinks about turning around.

Walking inside to the living room, Marie asks, "How are you doing Lynn?"

"I'm ok mamma. What did you want?"

"Well, I've been doing a lot of thinking and…."

Before she can finish, Lynn interrupts her, "Get to the point mother."

"Well, if you want to get an attitude with me, I'm going to get to the point. I want you to get your girls back. I want to enjoy the rest of my life without stress, Lynn. I raised you and you need to raise yours."

Lynn stares at her mother for a few seconds and then asks, "Why mamma? You don't love your grandkids anymore?"

"Don't try that with me Lynn. You and I know that I love those girls with all of my heart. You need to learn some responsibility," she says sternly. Then looking up, she keeps on, "Why won't you take your sunglasses off? Never mind; I don't even want to know. I do know you need to leave that no good Bo alone and raise your daughters." As Marie says this, Lynn gets up and walks to a picture of the girls analyzing it.

The two are quiet for a few minutes then Lynn says, "I know responsibility. You just don't want my girls. Don't worry about it. I will get them for good this weekend. You old mamma. You lived your life already, but it's ok. I'm going to get them this weekend."

Lynn gets up to leave when the girls come running to the living room to hug her. Nichole is extra excited to see her mom, but Danielle is coy. Danielle feels remorseful and wishes she could do something, so she just sits and stares at her mom. It feels like a piece of her is lost.

"What's wrong with you girl?" Lynn asks Danielle in a sarcastic manner.

"Nothing. I'm ok mamma." She says putting her head down.

"Well whatever it is, you need to get over it because ya'll moving with me this weekend," she says walking towards the door.

Hearing this, Danielle chest caves in like she has been hit in the chest with a large fist. She looks at Marie and Marie turns her head looking away from her. Nichole on the other hand is happy and jumping up and down.

"Make sure they have their stuff ready," she says to Marie.

"Ok Lynn, but you should talk to them before you come to get them."

"Don't worry about that. Just have them ready when I come back," Lynn says turning to leave.

"Ok Lynn. Whatever you say."

When Lynn walks out the door, Danielle instantly asks, "Why do we have to move with her?"

"Well honey, Granmamma is old and can't do the things she used too. My body can't take the things it used too , baby. I know you might be a little upset, but your mother loves ya'll and she wants the best for you both." She explains.

"I'm not mad grandma. I want to go with mommy," Nichole says.

Danielle on the other hand is speechless. She turns away and goes upstairs to get her things ready. While getting ready, she starts to cry her eyes out. Nichole stays downstairs to finish talking to Marie. Danielle can only imagine how life is going to be now. The pain, the beatings, the smoke, the craziness. She gets angry and starts to throw things around the room. First her clothes then her toys. She just wants to know why her. She starts to shed tears. If a child can get become depressed, Danielle is in that state.

Lynn goes back to the hotel to tell Bo what Mare said. She is worried about what he is going to say, but she knows she has to handle her responsibility. If she doesn't, it will hunt her for the rest of her life. She reaches the door and enters her key. The red light comes on. She starts to panic. She bangs on the door desperately screaming Bo's name. She gets no answer. She walks to the office to tell the clerk that her key isn't working. The clerk notifies Lynn that the room was checked out of. Lynn can't believe her ears. Her world has stopped. Since her nerves are bad because of the crack she smokes, she starts to sweat and shake vehemently.

The clerk tries to calm her down but she doesn't accept the help. She can't think straight. She leaves the office and goes to a nearby park to gain some control of her thoughts and calm her nerves. Still shaking, she sits on the bench taking deep breaths. Her deep breaths seem to calm her briefly, but then her thought hits her like a windstorm. *What am I going to do now? Why the hell would he leave me now; all of a sudden? He is a no good, trifling peace of shit. He knows I don't have any place to go. Now I have to get these kids by myself, damn him.* She continues to sit on the bench with her rushing thoughts. She can't believe he just got up and left her without telling her. She tries to come up with a plan. Maybe she can move back with her mother. That would make life much easier. Everything would be perfect because she could put the crack rock down now, get a job, and find a nice place to live with her kids. She knows she doesn't have many options.

She looks up at the blue sky with tears in her eyes and realizes what she has to do. She decides that she will take the girls and move to Chicago to start over. *I'm not going to ask my mamma for shit. I'm going to do it myself; me and my God.*

Chapter 4

"Where we going mamma?" Nichole asks.

"We moving to Chicago to start a new life."

"With daddy?" Danielle asks.

"With no daddy. Only us," she replies with a smile on her face.

Immediately upon hearing this, Danielle gets the happiest she has been in a while. It's like a weight was lifted off of her shoulders. They are on the bus to Chicago. For Danielle, the ride is very peaceful. The girls have most of their things from Marie's house. For Lynne, the clerk at the hotel told her there wasn't anything left to give her, so she has nothing.

Starring out of the window, watching the trees and buildings pass by, Lynn thinks about the family she called on for help that denied her. She won't let that stop her. Lynn believes Chicago is full of opportunities, so she decides to start off in a shelter, get herself cleaned up, find a job. Hopefully, find a nice apartment to live in. She thinks to herself, *Yeah, things are going to get better for us. I know it is.*

Lynn is familiar with Chicago but not fluently. She knows more about the West Side of Chicago than the south side. She knows the west side is mostly black, so she chooses to start over in a shelter on the West Side of Chicago. Before she left Waukegan, she looked for shelters on that side and found one that caught her attention in the Garfield neighborhood on Lake street and Keeler avenue that houses females only.

Lake street gets very busy due to the overhead train. And since people commute to work on Lake street, Lynn feels that living on Lake will inspire her to get a job or she might meet someone that could give her a job. The family makes it to Lake street and Danielle is hypnotized by the big poles that hold the train up. They signify something to her.

The shelter is in the middle of the block with bars on the widows and front door. Lynn notices that from the outside, you wouldn't be able to know it is a shelter. It doesn't show the name like most places. Lynn likes it this way.

    Entering the shelter, there is a long hallway with white walls and brown shiny floors that leads to a big room where everybody sleeps. Lynn has to check them in at the front desk, so she tells the girls, "You girls go sit in the big room while I get us checked in."

    The two walk to the room as Lynn told them. Everything seems so big and different to Danielle. They are the only people there, so Danielle looks around to see what is there. The room has tables and chairs for eating; one big television; toys for the kids in the corner. Beds are stacked on top of each other in another corner. She doesn't know what to make of it. She heard from her mother that this was a "shelter," but she really doesn't know what it means. The two sit in the chairs silently in the chairs waiting on their mother to come back.

"Ok girls. We are all checked in. We have to leave until night time," Lynn says.

"Why mamma? What is a shelter?" Danielle asks.

"Well, it's a place people go when they don't have their own place to live where they have to pay rent. We can stay here for free until mommy gets a job then we can get our own place. Only girls live her too baby. They feed us and everything," Lynn explains.

"Ok mamma."

"It's going to be ok," while holding Danielle's hand.

Danielle shakes her head in agreement, but she really doesn't know what's going on; her thoughts are at a disarray. Nothing makes sense to her. Everything is why. *Why don't we have a house to live in? Why do we have to live in a shelter? I wish I was never born.*

The three sit there for a short while talking about their plans for the future.

"First, I'm going to get you both in school. Then, I'm going to look for a job. Yea…yea, I know we gone be alright. I know we are," Lynn tells the girls, but really.

Lynn doesn't lie to the girls. She follows her plan. She gets the girls in school, slows up on the drugs, and starts a job at the corner store on Lake Street and Pulaski as a cashier. Things start to look up for Lynn while Danielle tries to get adjusted to the shelter life.

It's hard for Danielle though. While going to a new school, she starts to get bullied. They roast her on the way she dresses and smells because the other girls have all of the latest shoes and clothes. Danielle has the hand me downs from the other kids in the shelter. They also talk about how she looks because she is light skinned. The kids make it appear that having lighter skin with long hair is ugly.

It gets so bad, they start to call her white and throw things at her. She tells Lynn, but all Lynn tells her is to ignore them. She tries ignoring them, but the taunting gets worse. Some kids even start to spit on her during recess. Now she knows she is ugly.

However, not all of the kids in her class tease her by the way. The girl that sits directly behind her named Ashley doesn't. Ashley feels for Danielle because she used to get roasted and bullied before Danielle came. Before long, the two become friends.

Ashley stays one block from Lake street on Maypole avenue and the school is two blocks from Lake street on West End, the two walk to school together. They become real close and they stick together in school.

Thus, while in recess one day, Ashley explains to Danielle what she has to do to stop them from picking on her.

"When I first came, they was doing me like they doing you now. No matter what I did, they always messed with me…"

"Why?" Danielle asks.

"You know the fat one?"

"Yea."

"Her name is Brandy but I call her Big Bubbles," she says while smiling. Danielle smiles too. Ashley continues. "She knows she ugly so she picks on us. When I found that out, I roasted her so bad that she cried then everybody else left me alone."

"For real?" Danielle asks.

"Yea, in the middle of recess too. It was so raw. You should try it." Ashley tells Danielle.

Hesitant for a while, Danielle says, "I don't know Ashley. What if she tries to fight me?"

"Fight her back. Even if you don't win, she won't think you a punk."

"I guess you are right," Danielle says unconfidently.

"Ok, so the next time she starts something with you, just hit her in the nose as hard as you can. Make her bleed if you can"

"I'm going to get into trouble if I do that." Danielle says.

"Yea, but not forever and Bubbles will leave you alone because she will respect you. I promise she will." Ashley says.

"I don't know about that."

"Well, keep letting her punk you then." Ashley says shaking her head.

Danielle doesn't respond. She knows that she should do something because she is tired of getting picked on. After thinking about it, she decides the next time Brandy picks on her she will do what Ashley suggests.

It doesn't take long for Brandy to pick on her again. This time, Brandy spits on her while they are on bathroom break in the hallway. Danielle looks at Ashley for a second, turns and punches Brandy hard in the nose. It hurts Brandy so much that she can't scream. She falls down and folds up like a lazy boy sofa. She then jumps up and runs inside to tell the teacher with blood dripping through her hand down her shirt. When Danielle sees this, she looks at Ashley and smiles.

Danielle get's suspended, but she gains respect from the other girls. Ashley and Danielle become best friends after this, and a different Danielle comes out after this. She promises herself to never let someone hurt her without her putting up a fight.

Chapter 5

~Years Later~

"I know you never did this before shorty but shit will work out," Kurt says while taking a pull from his perfectly rolled blunt.

"Yea, it will be good. I wouldn't even put you in harms way tho," he continuies while handing her the blunt.

"I know, but what if I get caught?" she asks.

"Shorty, don't even think like that. That's how they catch you. Think like you can never get caught cuz you not gone get caught."

The two are sitting in Kurt's green Cadillac with the big shiny rims on Van Buren and Karlov. Kurt is the number two man on the block under his brother Birdy.

Danielle met Kurt four months ago walking down Puaski to the gas station. He pulled up in his nice car; she couldn't resist him. She knew he sold drugs for money, but he seemed like a nice person. Now he wants her to sell drugs for him because he knows her situation. He knows that she barely has a place to stay because her mom is on drugs. He sells it to her. He knows Danielle needs the money. He says it's helping her out.

The two finish smoking the blunt while Kurt continues to explain the hustling life.

"Look right. You a female; the police not gone expect you to be selling drugs. Plus, you look good so they really not going to think nothing." he says with a smile on his face.

"I guess, she says smiling back at him.

"But don't get it twisted, these K town streets aint shit to play with," he says sternly.

She looks at him and shakes her head, "I know it's messed up out here."

"I'm telling you shorty. Shit will be decent. You my boo. I won't let nothing happen to you," he says grabbing her thigh.

At this moment, one of the workers on the block comes to the car and asks for more work. When Kurt reaches in his pants to give the worker a bundle, Danielle gets a slight rush. She feels like a queen to a boss. She likes this feeling. The two discuss what money to bring back to him then he takes her to Ashley's house.

Danielle is excited and can't wait to tell to tell Ashley, but then again, she can't tell Ashley because she might not agree with it. She goes in to tell Ashley that she is thinking about selling drugs, she over hears Ashley's mom talking about her. She stops by the door to listen.

"I don't know what that girl is going to do, but she better do something because I'm going to need some money," Ashley mom says.

"I know mamma, but she trying. Look at all the stuff she been thru," Ashley says.

"I hear all of that but she needs to do something. I been thru stuff too. I can't tell the bill collectors that," Ashley mom responds.

"Ok mamma. I will….."

Before Ashley can finish her sentence, Danielle walks in the room with a confused look on her face. At that instant, she walks out the room and goes into the room she sleeps in. Ashley follows because she knows Danielle heard them, so she tries to explain.

"It aint what you think. She just need a little help with the bills in stuff," Ashley says.

"I know. I heard her. I got a plan."

"What's yo plan?" Ashley asks.

"I'm about to hustle on Van Buren, save some money, and get my own shit," Danielle says.

"With Kurt and them?" Ashley asks.

"Yea. I talked to him today about it and I was just coming to tell you."

Turning her head looking Danielle in the eyes, "Are you sure you want to sell drugs?"

"I mean, I don't have no choice. I need money and Kurt and them getting money. Have you seen his car?

"Yea, I saw it but still. They are always into it with somebody because of that damn Pee-Wee and Maniac. I know you hear them gun shots every other day," Ashley says.

"I don't know about all of that. I do know I need some money." Danielle replies.

"I guess. If that's what you really want to do. Do you girl," Ashley says.

"I am," Danielle says walking in the front room.

Danielle walks in the front room thinking to herself, *I really just made my mind up that quick? I guess so As long as I stay with Kurt. I will be good."*

So the next day, she wakes up early to go on Van Buren to execute her plan. She has to mentally prepare herself for the drug game, but she is determined to make money. It is the end of summer, but yet it's hot. When she reaches the block, she doesn't see Kurt. There are a few people on the block that she knows. She walks up to Pee-Wee, "Where Kurt at?" She asks.

"He was here but he made a move. What up tho?"

"He said he gone let me hustle today."

"I'm running the block right now. I can give you a pack," he says flaming up a cigarette looking both ways down the block.

When she hears this, she gets confused and nervous. She says, "imma wait for him cuz he is going to tell me something before I start."

"aight bet. If you change yo mind. Let me know." He says.

"ok."

She sits on Ray Ray's porch, one of the guys, in the middle of the block and observes how things operate. Her eyes are wide open like a window. She first sees from Pee-Wee that the runner passes out the drugs to te person that will sell them to the customer. Being that it is morning, there are only a few cars pulling up asking for "Blows." She doesn't know what that means but she is going to wait to ask Kurt. She notices that there is a certain kind of look the people that do blows have; slurred speech, raspy voice, swayed movement like the trees in the wind. All she can think to herself is *I have to win. I can do this.*

While pumping herself up, Kurt pulls up with a big smile on his face and screams out, "You ready to get this money baby?"

She smiles from ear to ear jumping off the porch like a frog yelling, "Hell yea. I been ready. I was waiting on you. Shidd you the one playing."

"Man hell naw. Come ride with me real quick," he says.

"ok."

She gets in the car looking at his lap; she sees a gun and a knot full of cash, it turns her on. He drives off to discuss business.

"Go in the glove compartment box and get me a blunt," he tells her.

She gets a blunt from the pile of pre-rolled ones and lights one up.

"So what do I have to do," she says inhaling the smoke.

She acts like she doesn't know anything to get Kurt's full attention.

"Look right, I'm going to give you the packs myself and I want you to serve the costumers. You can stand on the block and watch them hustle and when you feel like you ready, let me know," he tells her.

"That's cool. I will do that for like a hour then imma hustle," she says.

"Aight bet," he says.

"O yea, I forgot. No matter if you have something on you or not, always watch out for the police," he tells her taking a pull from the blunt.

They ride around to finish smoking the blunt. He then parks on Van Buren and Karlov because Danielle gives him a inkling that she wants to have sex. He takes her to his grandmother's house on

Gladys and Karlov. It doesn't last long. It never last long. When they finish, they walk to Pulaski to hustle.

They stand on the corner right beside each other. Cars are pulling up asking for "blows." She even sees white people pulling up asking for blows that looks like they own big time companies. She remembers that she wanted to ask Kurt what blows means so she asks him.

"What blows mean again?" she asks quietly.

"That's what we call our dope or our heroin. They go for ten a pop." He says looking both ways.

"O, ok." She says.

Everybody is out on the block now too. They all look like they are getting money and having fun. Being on the block is like a movie she has to be in, so she asks Kurt to make her a star and that's what he does.

Chapter 6

As a result of her wanting to be a block star, she finally tells Kurt she is ready, so the next day, they meet in the ally to give her the packs. Before he gives her the drugs, he tells her again.

"Always watch out or the police. When you see em, call out MJ or Lights Out. This what everybody calls out too. If you hear one of them names, know they police in the area."

"Ok, what should I do when they are around?" she asks.

"Go in Booms on Pulaski, or walk off so they won't see you and if you have something on you, stash that shit so they won't find it. Aight?"

"Yea, I got it," she says.

At this time, he gives her two packs.

"Count them real quick. It's supposed to be fourteen in each pack." he tells her.

She counts them and they are all accounted for.

"When you done with them two, turn the money in to Maniac. Imma give you two more."

"Ok, I got you," she says.

At that instant, she is on Van Buren and Pulaski ready to get money. While reaching the corner, she gets an overwhelming feeling. It's impalpable then suddenly somebody pulls up, "Who got the blows?"

She doesn't respond at first, then he yells again, "Who got the blows girl?"

A strong voice that's different for the previous one yells out, "Aye baby girl? Don't you got the work?"

Danielle snaps out of it and says, " yeah, I got it."

"You got a customer shorty. Keep yo head up out here." Maniac tells her.

"Ok," she says then she asks the customer, "how many you want?"

"Give me five," the man says.

Danielle takes the pack out where everybody can see it, opens it, and serves her customer.

The man gives her a fifty dollar bill and drives off. Putting the money in her pocket, she feels some type of way.

"Aye baby girl? I know you new to this hustling shit, but act like you know you selling drugs. Don't be pulling yo pack out all in the open like that. Turn around, pull you stash out, then serve. Don't get us locked up out here. If you gone keep something on you, put it I your crack." Maniac tells her.

"Ok. I got you."

She tries to listen to him, but costumers are pulling and walking up so fast, she has no other choice but to keep it in her hand. Before she knows it, she sells all twenty four blows. She is excited. Even though she has to turn in two hundred and forty dollars, she now has money in her pocket.

She is ready to sell more. It comes easy to her. She leans on the wall watching everybody else thinking to herself. *If it goes like this all the time, I can make enough money to get my own place. I might be able to get my own car. This is what I need.*

Looking down the block, she sees Kurt pulling up. She flags him down shyly asking him, "Can I get two more packs?"

"You done?"

"Yea, I been done," she says.

"Hell yeah, get in."

They ride around the block so he can give her two more packs then he drops her off. As her feet touch the pavement with drugs again, she feels like a thug. It's like a transformation. She posts up on the corner making things appear like she has hustled for a long time.

Even though it's her first day, she catches on fast. When cars pull up, she is there.

"How many you want?"

When customers walk up, she is there.

"How many you want?"

She wants Kurt to know that she has always had hustling in her blood. She sells the two packs faster then before because of a white customer that bought one whole pack. When Kurt sees this, he gives her four more packs instead of two. Doing like Maniac said, she stashes three packs and puts the others in her crack.

During rush hour or from 3:00pm to 7:00pm, the block really pick up. It goes so fast that shen she is done with her four packs, she calls it a day going in with $180.00. When Ashley sees her, she has the biggest smile on her face.

"What you smiling about?" Ashley asks.

"I hustled today and made one eighty. That shit moving!"

"So you really selling drugs on Van Buren with them huh?"

"Yeah, I need the money Ashley. I'm good. Let me do me."

"Yeah aight," Ashley responds.

"After tomorrow, I can give your mamma some money."

"I guess Danielle."

The two finish talking and Danielle goes into the room she sleeps in thinking to herself, *this hustling shit was made for me.*

She closes her eyes falling asleep to get ready for the next day. She doesn't want to do anything else but get money.

Chapter 7

"Blows, Blows, Park," Danielle screams out to the cars driving past on Pulaski. At this time in the morning, her drugs are selling fast. She was the first to come on the block with Kurt to open up. The two post up together selling back and forth. They have a sort of block bond.

"Aye shorty; you sell three packs, I sell three packs until another worker comes to work," he says.

"And when I get the pack, you better keep your head up for MJ," he continues.

"Ok, I got you baby," she says.

That's what she does. When Kurt sells, she has her head sticking out like a giraffe looking for the police, and Kurt does the same thing until other people come to work. After that, they take a break to eat, smoke, and have sex. For them, this becomes a habitual activity.

On this day, Danielle starts to see more money for herself. She is on the block every day. Her clothes and shoe game steps up too. By Danielle being on the block every day, she becomes cool with all of the guys. They see she is a hustler. They start to take a liking to her. To her, they're just being cool. She doesn't notice when Maniac is always trying to give her weed and smoke with her after they finish hustling; Or when Frilly constantly tries to drink Remy Martin with her when he comes on the block.

From their actions, Kurt starts acting different. He starts telling her she can't do certain things with the guys on the block. No smoking with them, no drinking with them to nothing with them. To Danielle, their just being cool; basically showing block love.

To please Kurt, she stops smoking and drinking with them. She only comes on the block to hustle, but that still doesn't seem to be enough for Kurt. He starts to get overly committed to stopping Danielle from what it looks like any interaction with any of the guys.

On this occurrence, Kurt rides down the block, jumps out his car saying things like, "Why you come on the block with that on? Why you looking at Maniac like that? Why you smiling at Rock like that? What you like him or something?"

"No Kurt, I'm just being nice. We all hustle together. It's not like that baby," she says back to him.

"Yeah, aight. Keep playing with me shorty. Imma knock yo head off."

"I'm not on shit with any of them. I promise," she says holding his hand.

Danielle tries to pretend like she's not embarrassed; like Kurt didn't jump out if front of everybody telling her what she can and can't do. But really, she's dumbfounded and sort of hurt. The incident makes her think about her father. She knows Kurt isn't like her father though. Kurt is better then him. Kurt loves her. He just gets a little excited at times. She knows how to calm him down.

"When I finish this pack, we gon smoke a dro bag and have sex. Ok baby?" she asks Kurt looking him in his eyes.

He pretends that he doesn't want to do what she just asked. He looks down the block both ways, he gets some of the other guys attention asking them how much work they have left, and he is trying his best to avoid her.

"Ok baby?" She asks again.

"Yea, I guess shorty," he says with an attitude.

"Ok baby. You staying on the block until I finish this pack?

"Na, I'm about to go get Frilly from the barbershop." He says.

"ok, come back and get me. Imma be done by then." She tells him.

"I got you." He says walking back to his car.

Danielle smiles then she gets back on point. The people that live on the block are looking at her like she is doing something strange. Some of them look at her shortly then turns their head; some are shaking their head. The reason why is that they see people come and go. They know how Kurt is. They remember what happened to the last girl Kurt had working on the block. They guys off the block was having sex with her in a vacant building ramming all types of objects inside of her because she was slipped some embalming fluid or what they call "Wack." It wasn't solely Kurt's fault though. He just didn't stop them. After that harsh undertaking, the girl was doing blows and eventually was nowhere to be found.

Danielle doesn't know the real reason why they're looking at her, so she looks at them thinking to herself, *they can't judge me. They dirty anyway. They need to be out here getting money with me* while *walking* to the curve with the block's routine gab.

"Blows, blows, park."

Kurt comes back to get her and they go to a hotel to have passionate sex. They get back to hustling the next day.

Chapter 8

"I know dude still around here man. He just served," Kurt says to the three people in the car with him while he turns the corner on Karlov.

"I know G. I just saw him too," Ice Mike says staring out of the back window intensely.

"We gon see him. Don't trip G," Lil Mello says calmly.

"I know we is. I aint tripping," Kurt responds.

"I hope we do cuz he whooped my favorite customer," Danielle says.

The four are riding around the block in the middle of the day looking for a guy with a grey Nike hoodie, a Chicago Bulls snap back cap, black Levi jeans, and all white Nike Air Force Ones that served a known customer some fake drugs this morning. Whoopin is a no-no on Van Buren and Karlov. Kurt doesn't play that. They ride around a few more blocks. Driving north up Karlov, east on Jackson, and south down Pulaski past Gladys when Lil Mello spots the guy walking through the ally.

"Aye G, there he go," he says while exiting the back of the car while it's still moving.

"Hold up G, let me pull over," Kurt screams out.

Kurt pulls in the ally and jumps out; Ice Mike follows him. Danielle stays in the car staring at them. Lil Mello chases the guy down and catches him in the middle of the ally. He pins the guy on a garage and starts to punch him in the face.

"You want to serve whoops on the block huh nigga?" Lil Mello asks him while he is punching him in the face. Lil Mello is trying to take it easy on him then Kurt runs up open hand slapping the guy.

"You think we sweet huh?" Kurt asks in his angry voice but still seeming reserved.

"Na Kurt. I don't think that man. I didn't do nothing." The guy says nervously.

"Yes you do," Ice Mike says punching him in the gut.

While he is slightly bent over, Danielle walks up, digs in his pockets, and walks back to the car. The three guys look at each other, but they don't say anything. They act like it is normal; like they did it before.

Breaking the silence, Kurt sees a stick on the ground by the garage; he picks it up and demands him to "Stay from off Van Buren nigga!"

He then hits him in the head with the stick making a horrendously loud sound, "SMACK!"

"This my block!" Kurt says without losing his cool.

The three stay around long enough to see the guy's body wobble to the ground and they run back to the car speeding off towards Congress a block after Van Buren where Lil Mello lives and sells weed.

They park on Congress in front of Lil Mello house in the middle of the block to smoke a blunt and let the police down just in case somebody seen or heard something.

While breaking the blunt down, Kurt asks, "How much money dude had on him?"

"He had 4 hundred on him. He had to be whoopin. Nobody selling like that but us." she says.

"We know he was whoopin. The customer named everything dude had on; from top to bottom. We got em so shit don't even matter now. Aye, give me 2 hundred, give them two 50 and you take the rest," he says.

"Ok. I got you baby."

While they are breaking the money down, and rolling up the blunt, two of the guys that Lil Mello hustles with on Congress, Ronchy and Big I walk up to the car.

Kurt lets down the window, they shake hands, "what up with yall gangstas?"

"Chilling big homie," they respond together.

"I hear you, " he says letting the window back up.

Ice Mike speaks then Lil Mello gets out of the car, "what up ya'll?"

"Nothing for real. We trying to see what you about to do," Ronchy says.

"I was about to smoke this blunt with Kurt and em and hustle for a minute longer. We just had to beat this dude ass on Van Buren for whoopin."

"When? Just now?" Ronchy asks.

"Yea G. Kurt came to get some weed, so I jumped in with him and baby girl in the front seat told him somebody was whoopin so we got on it." Lil Mello says.

"That's crazy though. I just walked down Pulaski," Big I says.

"He probably still laying in the ally and shit," Lil Mello says.

While they are talking, Ronchy is looking in the front seat at Danielle. He acts like he is looking for the blunt. He likes what he sees. So he asks, "Who is shorty in the front seat anyway G?"

"She hustling on Van Buran. I think Kurt messing with her. Man, everybody over there might be messing with her. You know how that go," he says laughing a short bit.

"Aw, she look good though. We need to get here over here to hustle for us," Ronchy says.

Interrupting them, "Yall trying to hit this blunt?" Kurt asks.

"Hell yeah," Big I says.

Big I hits the blunt twice then gives it back. Then, the three stands by the car for a short while longer selling weed until Kurt drives off.

Kurt takes Ice Mike and Danielle on Van Buran. He goes to get more drugs for the block. Danielle is indeed high and is sitting on Ray Ray's porch thinking about the guy pockets she went into. *I would do it to anybody who plays with my money or Van Buran. He lucky I didn't tell Kurt to shoot his ass. I know he would've done it for me. I'm his main bitch. I come first.*

Chapter 9

Long days and short nights for Danielle. "Same Dope, different shake," as Kurt likes to say. The block is a full time job. She's like the manger; a block manger that is. Kurt is part owner. Van Buran makes the equivalent amount of money "real businesses" do; the legal ones. On any given day, the block can make 10 to 15k. Everybody sees that the block is doing numbers.

The person on security stays with new clothes on because his job isn't that hard. The pack worker stays with new clothes on, and some of them even buy cars that faintly work. The runner's stay with new clothes on, fair cars, and they barely have to stand on the block. The main runners have flashy cars. Of course, Danielle is the exception to the trend.

She runs the block, but it's like she's there to make Kurt rich. She's getting good money. She's buying designer clothes. She's smoking good dro. She has two cell phones. She can have a car, but she doesn't know how to drive. So, wit the money she makes that can go on a car, she gives it to Kurt. He not only upgraded his green Cadillac to an all white 1961 Lincoln Continental with the suicide doors, 22inch rims, and a amazing sound system. He also has an up to date Cadillac with bigger rims than the last one. It's his everyday car.

The money that can go on an apartment, she gives it to Kurt while she still lives with Ashley. He has a condo in the suburb Oak Brook west of Chicago. He knows he living the hustling dream. While riding around the hood smoking dro, he will say things like,

"I was born to do this hustling shit! This shit runs through my blood baby girl," blowing the smoke out of his nose.

"We built this shit from ground up. They know Van Buran getting money. Look at they face when they see me ride past. Me and my niggas kings," He says.

Danielle loves when Kurt talks like this. It makes her get a tingly feeling in her pants. She will do anything for him. Her love for him runs deep.

Nonetheless, Kurt isn't fabricating his life when he says people know he's getting money. People really know they're getting money because after hustling hours, they come from all over the city to hang out. It's like they have to be around money.

On one side of Van Buran, a crowd of people in a circle with money in their hands and big clouds of smoke over their heads might be yelling, "Shoot that money Joe! That ain't yo point. Crap out nigga. Don't make me bust yo head out here nigga!"

A few feet from them, crowds of people get a kick out of standing next to the flashiest car on the block at the time with clear cups and blunts in their hands; in addition to the sounds of Young Jeezy playing loud in the background; Jeezy motivates the thugs. Kurt loves his music. It's like he talks to him when he raps. He recites the lyrics when they really apply to him, *"The world is yours, and everything in it, it's out there, get on your grind and get it. Hands in the air. Sky's the limit!* Aye G, Jeezy speaks the truth. I came from nothing, now look what I got. I'm hood rich niggas. I did it, na, we did it! This shit ain't gone never stop. I might buy the block!"

When they have the block functions, Danielle doesn't really get involved. She will sit on the red fire hydrant on the corner smoking a dro blunt, looking at the way Kurt acts thinking to herself. She's happy for Kurt . His hard work paid off. She loves to see him shine, but she hates to see the attention it brings. She sees how the females flock around him like birds because he has bread. She sees how dudes from other blocks looks at him when they ride past.

She even sees how some of his friends envy him. She tries to warn him, but he just brushes her off. *He will see one day. Maybe I'm tripping, but I know what I see. They hating on my baby. They better not play with him though. I know he will kill something if he had too.*

While she's sitting on the fire hydrant getting high, Kurt is in the backseat of his Lincoln receiving oral sex from one of his broads. She finishes her blunt and walks to Ashley's house.

Chapter 10

"Blows, blows, park. Come get this shit. It's the best dope in Chicago," Danielle says while customers are walking up to get served.

"Yea, I know sweetheart. I heard about this dope all the way in Indiana. Give me two jabs," he says jogging to Danielle.

"It is!." She says while running to her stash to get two jabs. She tries to serve him quickly to get to the other customers. She wants to make all the money today.

While she has her back turned, she hears a familiar voice that says, "Let me get one."

She turns around and it's her father, Bo. He is real thin; appearing like he hasn't eaten in a couple of days. His cheeks are sunk in like he has something sour in his mouth. He reminds her of a zombie. She instantly goes into a stupor; a state of speechless mental confusion. She somberly stares at Bo. Bo stands there staring back at her until Maniac walks up, "you good shorty?"

She doesn't answer the first time, so he asks again, " Lil mamma! You good?"

Snapping out of her stupor, "I'm aight."

She walks off towards Karlov trying to mentally put things together. Bo follows her.

"You gone let me get one for free?" Bo asks standing on the corner.

"What?"

"I need one baby. I'm dope sick," he says.

"I'm not giving you nothing. Leave me alone," she says.

"I'm yo daddy! If it wasn't for me, you wouldn't be here. Give me one of them blows girl!" He demands.

"You saying that like that's a good thing. I didn't ask to be here. Sometimes I wish I was dead," she tells him.

"Girl, I don't have time for this shit I need to get high right now. Don't make me take it."

"You not taking shit from me and I'm not selling you shit either! Go buy it from somewhere else. Go bout your business." she tells him.

"Girl, if you don't give me a blow, we gone have some problems" he says. Bo's addiction takes over and he grabs her by the arms trying to go into her pockets.

"Get off me! What the hell you doing?" Danielle screams out.

"I only wanted one, but imma take all of your drugs now," he says wickedly.

As he is trying to rummage through her pockets, Maniac and one of the other guys are standing on the block looking at what's gong on. This is what Maniac thrives on. He takes this opportunity to flex.

"Aye G, watch this," he tells his homie standing next to him. He runs into the vacant lot to the trunk of his Chevy to get a Louis Ville slugger with black tape wrapped around the handle. He runs back to the block creeping up behind Bo. Danielle is so emotional that she isn't paying attention to what is about to happen.

Without saying a word, Maniac swings the bat connecting with Bo's head like it is a baseball "SMACK!" Instantly showing the white meat.

This sends vibrations through the entire block. Bo falls slowly face first; Maniac runs to his car and drives off.

Danielle stands over him for a short while not knowing what to feel. The blood starts to gush out of his head. This makes her snap out of her trance. Bo isn't moving. She doesn't know what to do. Her mind is zooming, so she decides to buy some Dro off Congress. Smoking always helps her calm down. She runs through the lot to find Lil Mello.

Chapter 11

When she makes it on Congress, there are a few people standing in front of Lil Mello's house. She is nervous, so her hands and lips are shaking. Taking steps towards the small crowd, she hears the sirens on Van Buren. This makes her skin crawl. It makes her want to hide under a rock.

Breathing heavily, "Let me get a dub."

"What happened on VB?" Ronchy asks.

"I don't know. I think they beat up a hype or some shit," she says.

Ronchy runs to his stash to retrieve a dub sack. While waiting, Lil Mello walks up.

"What up shorty? What happened on VB?"

"I think they beat up a hype. I came to get a bag then I heard the sirens," she says.

"O, aight."

Ronchy walks up with a smile on his face looking at Lil Mello, "here shorty." She pays him then he asks, "You need a blunt?"

"Yeah, you got one?"

"I got one, but you have to let me blow it with you. Cool?"

"Ummm, I guess," she says with doubt.

"Where you want to smoke at?"

She knows Kurt can't see her smoking with him so she asks, "You don't have a place to smoke at?"

"Yeah, we can smoke in Lil Mello crib."

"Ok," she says.

The two go on the second floor to Lil Mello house to smoke. Lil Mello is only sixteen but he has his own apt. His mom owns the building so she gave him the second floor apartment. He does everything out of it. It's the trap house.

The two enter the apartment through the front door.

"Sit on the couch. Make your self at home," Ronchy says.

"Ok," she says shyly.

She sits on the couch while Ronchy proceeds to break the blunt down to roll up.

"You not from around here right?" Ronchy asks.

"No. I'm from Waukegan but I been out here for a minute," She responds.

"I can tell you not from out here tho."

"How can you tell?" she asks cracking a smile.

"I just can. I was born and raised in K Town. I can tell shorty," he says lighting up the blunt.

"I guess," she says.

Sitting on the couch, her mind is moving at a fast pace about what just happen and what she is going to do. She really just wants to hit the blunt. When Ronchy passes her the blunt, she takes the longest pull from it and leans back in the couch.

"You need that shit huh?" Ronchy asks her.

"Hell yeah. Shit been real crazy on VB," she responds exhaling the weed smoke.

"I feel you. Why you sell dope anyway? You to pretty for that shit."

"It's a long story but the dope moves fast. What getting money for ugly girls?"

"No I'm not saying that. I just know how it go if you get caught, them people not gone play with you," Ronchy says.

"I know, but I need the money. Nobody give me shit. I do it all on my own," she says passing him the blunt.

Hitting the blunt, "I hear you shorty. We not doing numbers like VB, but we eating off the weed and it's less time if you get caught. If you ever want to switch it up, you can get down with us."

"Ok. I will think about it."

"Even if you don't hustle with us, you can always come hang out on the block. I see something different in you. I would like to get to know you better and shit," he says touching her leg.

He startles Danielle causing her to jump a small bit. She is in complete abashment.

"My bad shorty. I'm not trying to scare you. I just know it's something different about you and I want to find out what it is. I'm not trying to hurt you. Trust me." he says.

"Ummm, I don't know about that. I go with Kurt and I know he wouldn't like that," she tells him.

"I understand shorty. Just know I'm feeling you. Imma leave it at that. though"

When they finish the blunt, Ronchy walks her outside. She walks past Lil Mello giving him the head nod. She walks toward Van Buren thinking about what Ronchy said. With the weed making her paranoid, she thinks to herself.

I really don't know what to do. What if he right? What if I get caught? I don't want to go to jail. I don't want Kurt to think I'm scared either. He the reason why I'm eating. I don't want him to be mad at me. Maybe I should talk to Kurt.

Suddenly, Kurt pulls up, "Aye shorty, get in. We been looking for you."

Chapter 12

"What happened on the block?" Kurt asks.

"Maniac smacked some hype across the head with a bat because he was trying to go in my pockets" she says.

"Awe, you good? He didn't get shit right?" He says more concerned about his money and drugs.

"Naw, he didn't have a chance too. Maniac ran right up on him."

"O, aight. Get back on the block then. The police gone. I need that Pac money so I can buy me a new Oyster perpetual Rolex," he says.

"Ok, baby. I have like two packs left. I need another bundle."

"Imma bring it to you," he says.

"Ok, baby."

She gets back on the block like she was told with thoughts of getting caught in the back of her mind. Her thoughts of getting booked don't stop her from hustling hard though. She wants Kurt to have everything he desires. She always goes hard on the block, but this time, she turns it up a notch. Going on the block earliest. Staying on the block the latest. All grind mode to get Kurt rich.

Danielle isn't the only one that turns up the notch however. Maniac and Frilly turns up too, but not on selling drugs. They turn up on rival gangs that think Van Buran and Pulaski is soft or can be played with. Kurt sends and pays for the hits.

Following orders, the two will go in broad daylight with no masks on and shoot rivals block up, not caring who they hit, and go back to Van Buran like nothing happened. They need to show that they are heartless and anybody can get it.

Danielle really doesn't know the magnitude of what's going on with the gun action that has been taking place, so she doesn't know that she should be more careful when she is on the block.

However, the guys know that they have to be alert on the block with guns ready, but when they are shooting craps, their minds are focused only on the dice and money. Even the person that has the gun to watch the ones that's shooting craps gets engaged in the game.

So on this day, with the sun shining bright, everybody on the block is lacking. Most of the guys are on the porch of the green house playing or watching the dice game. Kurt isn't on the block. Danielle and her security are on the corner serving focused on the money. They are unaware that a black Honda Accord is circling around the block scoping out the scene. Usually the guys on the block would have alerted they guy with the gun. Not today though. When the Black Honda Accord comes down the block for the fifth time, the car stops in front of the green house and opens fire, "bang bang bang bang, with a few more shots in succession.

Before they pull off, somebody yells out," This shit ain't never gonna stop until all ya'll dead."

Everybody scatters like roaches when the kitchen light comes on. Some people start yelling "Oh shit! Duck Joe! Damn Joe, it's a hit!"

Most jump off of the porch instantly, some crawl off the porch, and some of them even try grabbing others as a shield; complete chaos.

Danielle hears the shots, sees what is taking place, and freezes like she sees Medusa. Her security takes off like he is in a marathon. When they finish, they speed off not stopping for the stop sign. The guys slowly start coming back on the block.

Danielle is still frozen on the corner. Her security comes back and shakes her out of it. The guys slowly make it back to the block trying to check on everybody's well being.

When everybody makes it back to the block, they all check themselves to see if they were hit, when Frilly looks over and sees Maniac lying on the porch with his white tee red. His eyes are closed and to Frilly, it looks like he isn't breathing.

"Damn Joe! They got my man! Go get a car Joe. We gotta take him to Mount Sinai Joe," Frilly says panic-stricken.

One of the other guys, Tony, is standing next to Frilly says emotionally, "Hell naw Joe, call the truck to pick him up. He need them people working on him asap Joe." At this instant, people start coming to the porch screaming and hollering things like, "No! Get Help! Get Help. Maniac get up!"

Danielle walks to the porch wanting to see what happened for herself. When she sees Maniac stretched out with blood trickling out of his body with his naked face down on the porch, she starts crying and runs down the block to Congress.

She thinks to herself. *What the fuck did I get myself into. I just want to get money.*

Chapter 13

"You heard that shit? I think that was gunshots Joe. You got that 357 on you right?" Ronchy says to Lil Mello.

"Yea I got it," Lil Mello says putting his hand on the handle.

At that second, Ronchy looks down the block and sees Danielle running towards them crying. Ronchy runs towards her, "You ok baby girl?"

With her speech slurred and tears running down her face, she gets out, "Naw, they shot Maniac."

"What? He good?"

"I don't know. He was laid out on the porch then I ran over here," she says.

"Damn Joe! Aight, just go to Lil Mello crib and wait for us. We gone go around there and see what's up," he tells her.

The two run on Van Buran to see what's going on. She sits on Lil Mello's porch trying not to believe what just happened, but she knows it really did just happen. She has anxiety about the possibility of it happening to Kurt or even herself. As she is sitting there with her head in her lap, Kurt pulls up in the Lincoln.

"Aye baby girl, why you not on the block? Check it out!"

She gets up fast and runs to his car falling on the sidewalk because of her excitement and mental intricacy. The fall is feeble nonetheless. She gets up quickly hurdling in the car, "They shot Maniac!" she blurts out.

"What you talking about shorty?"

"They was all on the green house porch when this black car pulled up and starting shooting out of nowhere. Everybody ran all crazy, but when I walked down there, he was laid out on the porch with blood coming out of him," she tells him frantically.

"Why you over here tho?" He asks.

"I don't know. I couldn't take it, so I ran over here and told Lil Mello and them and they ran over there so I just sat on the porch."

Kurt then speeds off, turns right on Karlov and turns right on Van Buran making a rapid halt because of the ambulance and police that are in front of the green house.

"Shit! I know they didn't hit my man up!" He says banging on the steering wheel.

"He is going to be ok baby," Danielle says.

"Damn man! This shit crazy," he says.

He reverses the car and parks on Karlov.

"Man, Imma kill one of them boys," Kurt says grabbing his gun that's in his pants.

"Kill who? You know who shot him?"

"Man. This shit crazy Joe," he says trying not to answer her, but also thinking about what happened on the block.

"Kurt?"

"What!"

"Don't kill nobody baby. I'm hurt too. I just don't want you to go to jail. Let's do something else. This hustling shit is getting crazy," she tells him.

"What is you talking about? This is my life shorty. I feed this whole neighborhood. Hustling is how you eat; you forgot? This is what I am. I'm a hustler!" He says.

"I understand baby, but I don't want nothing to happen to you or me. We can put our money towards something else.

"Our money? This my money. You work for me. You talking crazy as fuck! Matter fact, get out my car," he says firmly.

"But Kurt I just want us to be saf…"

He cuts her off, "BITCH GET OUT BEFORE I PUT YOU OUT! DON'T YOU SEE THEY JUST GOT DOWN ON MY MAN? I AINT NEVER GOING LIKE THAT!"

With her head down, she slowly exits the car. Instead of going to Ashley's house, she walks to Lil Mello's house to see if they were back and to smoke some dro. She is in disbelief. She sits on Lil Mello's porch for a short while when Ronchy and Lil Mello walk up from the vacant lot.

"Yea shorty they did shot Maniac but they said he might make it," Ronchy says.

"For real?" she asks.

"Yea. They might of said that shit so we would be calm n shit. Everybody was standing around them."

"I hope so," she says.

"You want to smoke?" Ronchy asks her.

"Yea. Let's go upstairs tho. I don't want to sit outside right now. Them dudes might come back."

"They don't want it with us tho! We not about that talking, but aight, bet. I have a box of swishers. I want to take your mind off that shit," he says to her walking upstairs to get blazed.

Chapter 14

A few days pass ensuing Maniac's shooting and Danielle slows down hustling on Van Buran. She will pass out a few packs here and there, but not like before. She isn't talking to Kurt like she used too because he isn't around as much. She has a strong feeling that he is retaliating for Maniac even though Maniac didn't die. Frilly told her that they put him on something called a "shit bag," so he's resting up.

She doesn't want to get involved in shootouts, so she starts to hang out more on Congress. She feels safer from the other guys, but not from Kurt. She's afraid of Kurt, but she tries not to show it. He will seldom drive past and she will talk to him if he asks her to.

She will post up with them on Congress while they sell weed all the while taking a liking to Ronchy. She even sells weed for him without him even asking her to. She finds him different than others. He is a hustler, but with a heart. Plus, he says they are not beefing with anyone. This puts her at ease.

With passing weeks, she completely stops hustling on Van Buran and hustles on Congress full time with the weed. She also starts to get intimate with Ronchy because he treats her like a lady. He doesn't want her to hustle, but she insists just to show him that she's not lazy, so he lets her get down. Since Lil Mello lets the block sleep there whenever they want.

With that, she spends most nights with Ronchy there and at some later time, Kurt starts to really notice. It doesn't sit right with him. It's like she has been disloyal to not only the block, but to him. He also doesn't like when one his females stop talking to him without being able to dismiss them. And by now, Danielle knows that Kurt is an egotistical and controlling person, so she is on edge about that situation. She tries to warn Ronchy that Kurt is will do something to him or her, but Ronchy doesn't want her to worry about it.

"He not worried about us. He has bigger problems like them dudes that's shooting VB up," he tells her.

"I hear you but I know how he is. He rides past mean mugging me without even stopping anymore. But maybe I'm tweaking," she says.

"I can understand why you paranoid baby, but don't trip. We good. More than that, I want you to get back in school. I think that would be a better look for you. I'm even thinking about doing the school thing myself."

"I hope so baby. And I was just thinking about getting back in school. I want to help people thats been thru the stuff I've been through. I know you can do it too," she says.

"Well don't think about Kurt and think about all those people your are going to help. I'm here for you so don't trip," Ronchy says.

"I know baby. Thank you for being here for me," she says.

"Come on with all that. I'm doing what I'm supposed to. Just get on that asap."

"I am baby. I am," pushing him softly smiling from ear to ear.

As the time moves onward, Danielle makes sure she stops hustling and register for school.

Chapter 15

"Where you going boo?" Kurt says smiling while pulling up in his big body Lincoln.

"Why Kurt?"

"Man… stop playing with me for real shorty. Check it out real quick. I want to talk to you," Kurt says.

"What do you want? I'm trying to get to school?"

"Oh, you in school now?" He asks.

"Yea."

"I'm proud of you shorty. Real shit. I will take you."

"It's cool. I can get on the bus."

"Come on shorty. Aint nobody on that with you for real tho. I'm chilling. I want to make up for the last time you was in my car," he says.

"Kurt, I don't have time to be playing."

"I hear you shorty. For real. You know you still my boo no matter who you smashing on Congress," he says with a big smile on his face.

"See, you playing."

"Na, I quit. I quit. Get in tho."

Kurt pulls the car over letting Danielle get in. She is nervous but she plays it off. He lights up a blunt.

"Here hit this. It might help you learn something in school."

"Naw, I'm ok," she says.

"DAMN, you act like you don't know me no more. Stop acting brand new."

"Aint nobody acting brand new, dang. Let me hit it," she says.

So Kurt stays parked on Congress while the two hit the blunt before he takes her to school. While they are doing this, a guy creeps out of a gangway, comes around on Kurt's side with a black Glock 40 and shoots the car up. The bullets ring out like thunder.

"Bang, Bang, Bang. You thought we wasn't gone get yo ass."

Inside of the car, Kurt tries reaching for his gun but there are too many bullets to shoot back, so he struggles to block his face. He squirms around in is seat. He then utters out a loud, sharp cry out, "AYE, WHAT THE FUCK JOE. ON BREED JOE! NAW NAW!"

Danielle squirms around in her seat too in complete disbelief. She tries numerous of things, but all she can do is stop squirming and wait until it's over with. When it is over and complete silence comes, a total of seventeen bullets were released into Kurt's Lincoln.

Chapter 16

The pain of a gunshot is like none other. A bullet is hot and penetrates the skin that leaves holes you can see thru. It not only penetrates the skin, it pierces the soul also. A person is not the same after they have been shot.

When the thunderous sounds of the released bullets cease, Danielle tries to open her eyes and get out of the car but the pain is excruciating. She leans back in the seat. She then looks over at the driver seat. Kurt is slumped over the steering with half of his head on the dashboard. She tries to scream, but only gasps.

She then looks down at herself seeing blood gushing out of her body. The life that she has lived up to this point flashes before her eyes. She doesn't know what to do. She doesn't know what is going to happen. She then starts to shake vehemently. Her shaking leads to her eyes rolling in the back of her head. With this happening to her, she is still thinking to her self, *why? What if I just.....*

In the midst of her slipping in and out of consciousness, she hears sirens and loud piercing cries. Noooo! Not her! Not now Joe!"

"Why God? Why?"

"He dead Joe! They knocked his noodles out."

The doors are pulled open and they take Danielle out first because she shows signs of life. As her body moves, the pain increases. The sunlight makes it worse. She tries to look around, but she can't move. Her body feels really heavy. A loud familiar voice startles her but also gives her a cool sensation, "Danielle. Don't die on me baby. You gone make it! You strong baby. You strong," Ronchy pleads.

She wants to respond. She wants to say she is sorry. She wants to say she should've done something different, but all she can do is close her eyes and desire for her mother.

Closing Remarks

Kurt was shot ten times. He was dead on arrival. They had to scrape his head off of the dashboard to put it back together. He knew people wanted him dead because of the money he was making from selling drugs, but also because he killed friends of the person that killed him. His death could be said was his fate. He was twenty-three years old.

Danielle was shot five times. She survived the shooting but was paralyzed from the waist down. Before the shooting, she was registered for school and had a job interview the day after she was shot. When the reports came to the hood, she was said to be seventeen years old. Nobody really knew the real her. People in the neighborhood were distraught about Kurt's death, but about Danielle, all most of them had to say was, "At least she still living." Meanwhile, Lynne has no clue what happened to her daughter.

Author's Biography

Jermel Arcilicia Taylor is a Chicago native that now resides in Washington DC. He attends the University of The District Of Columbia majoring in Biology with plans to go to Medical School. His motivation comes from his family and all of things he has seen in this life.

Contact Information

jermelsraisondetre@gmail.com

www.jermelsraisondetre.com

NEXT WORKS

Brainwork 2: The Hustlers Handbook

DC Local – A Novel

College Boy – A Novel